Protecting
Our Planet

What Can We Do About the
ENERGY CRISIS?

Suzanne Slade

PowerKiDS
press.

New York

To Neil Milani, wind turbine engineer extraordinaire!

Published in 2010 by The Rosen Publishing Group, Inc.
29 East 21st Street, New York, NY 10010

First Edition

Editor: Amelie von Zumbusch
Book Design: Kate Laczynski
Photo Researcher: Jessica Gerweck

Photo Credits: Cover, p. 1 Paul Kennedy/Getty Images; back cover graphic © www.istockphoto.com/Jan Rysavy; p. 4 © Kevin Dodge/Corbis; p. 6 Gazimal/Getty Images; p. 8 Lester Lefkowitz/Getty Images; p. 10 © Lester Lefkowitz/Corbis; p. 12 Sam Royds/Getty Images; pp. 14, 18 Shutterstock.com; p. 16 Courtesy of Neil Milani; p. 20 Jim Karageorge/Getty Images.

Library of Congress Cataloging-in-Publication Data

Slade, Suzanne.
  What can we do about the energy crisis? / Suzanne Slade. — 1st ed.
    p. cm. — (Protecting our planet)
  Includes index.
  ISBN 978-1-4042-8081-6 (library binding) — ISBN 978-1-4358-2481-2 (pbk.) —
ISBN 978-1-4358-2482-9 (6-pack)
  1. Power resources—United States—Juvenile literature. 2. Energy development—United States—Juvenile literature. I. Title.
  TJ163.2.S6154 2010
  333.79—dc22
                              2008051935
                      38888000159321

Manufactured in the United States of America

CPSIA Compliance Information: Batch #WRW909101PK: For Further Information contact Rosen Publishing, New York, New York at 1-800-237-9932

CONTENTS

Powered by Energy

Energy makes people's lives easier. It runs our computers, washing machines, and TVs. Energy powers our cars. We need energy to heat and cool our homes. It also lights up the dark nights.

Most of the energy people use in the United States comes from burning fossil fuels, such as oil. Over time, people have used much of Earth's fossil fuel. If we keep using energy at the current rate, **scientists** say we will run out soon. This shortage is called the energy crisis. Today people are finding ways to **conserve** energy. They are also searching for new kinds of energy.

Fossil Fuels

About 85 percent of the energy used in the United States comes from fossil fuels. There are three kinds of fossil fuels. These are oil, coal, and natural gas. Oil is a thick, black liquid. Coal is a black rock. Natural gas is a colorless gas that naturally has no smell.

Each fossil fuel is used for different energy needs. Natural gas is often burned in ovens to cook food. It also heats homes and businesses. Oil and coal are burned in power plants to make the **electricity** we use in our homes, schools, and businesses. Our cars are powered by gasoline, which is made from oil.

Fuels Under the Ground

It takes **millions** of years for fossil fuels to form inside Earth. The fossil fuels we use today formed from things that lived many years in the past. The Sun's energy helps plants and animals grow. When plants and animals die, some sink deep into the ground. Over time, these remains break down and turn into fossil fuels. Coal forms from plants that once lived on land, while oil and natural gas come from tiny plants and animals that lived in the oceans long ago.

Earth's oil, coal, and natural gas have been stored in the ground for a long time. If we burn all of these fossil fuels, we cannot find or make more. Therefore, people must learn to use fossil fuels wisely.

Power plants produce many kinds of pollution,
including carbon dioxide, mercury, and sulfur dioxide.

Global Warming

When we burn fossil fuels to produce energy, they give off gases that **pollute** our air, water, and land. Pollution hurts all living things, including people. For example, pollution can give kids asthma, an illness that makes it hard to breathe.

The pollution made by burning fossil fuels is causing Earth's **temperature** to rise slowly. This is called global warming. Global warming changes animal habitats around the world. Deserts become hotter. The snowy North Pole gets warmer. Polar bears, elephants, and many other animals are in danger due to global warming.

DID YOU KNOW?

Earth's temperature has risen more than 1° F (.5° C) in the last 100 years. This change sounds small, but it has caused masses of ice, called glaciers, to melt and the sea to rise.

Saving Energy

Fossil fuels are nonrenewable. This means we cannot make more of these important fuels. To power our busy world, people must conserve the energy we have. Small changes in our everyday lives can make a big difference. Imagine how much gas would be saved if most people took a bus or train instead of driving their own cars.

There are many simple things you can do to save energy. Walk or ride your bike when you visit places that are nearby. Turn off lights when you leave a room. Take shorter showers to save hot water. By working together, we can conserve Earth's energy.

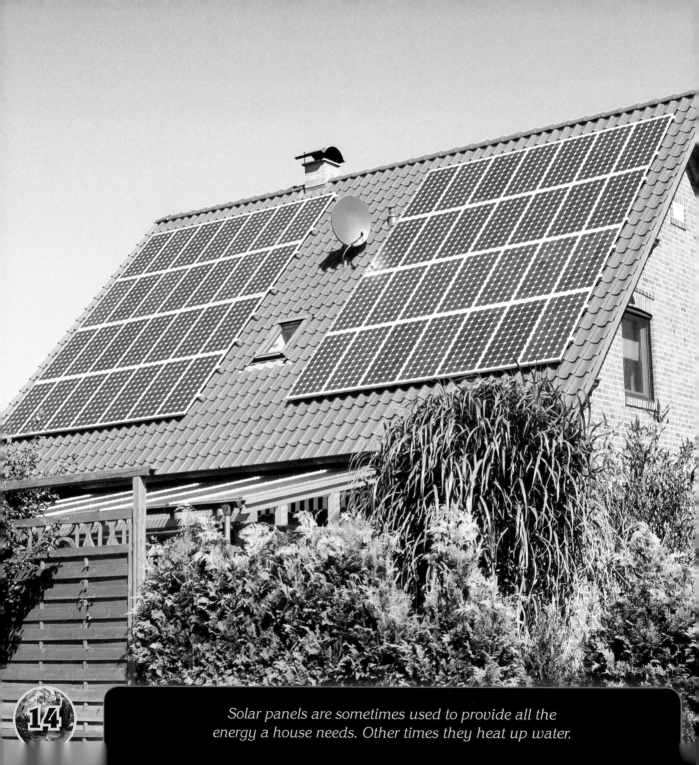

Solar panels are sometimes used to provide all the energy a house needs. Other times they heat up water.

Energy from the Sun

Turning to renewable energy, or energy made from natural **sources** that we cannot use up, cuts our fossil fuel use, too. For example, the Sun gives off solar energy in the form of heat and light. People have discovered ways to use solar energy.

Have you ever noticed large, black rectangles sitting on a roof? These shiny objects are solar panels. Solar panels trap the Sun's energy and turn it into energy people can use. Solar panels make electricity for houses and businesses. They produce power for cars, boats, planes, and even spaceships!

Wind farms are generally built in flat, windy places.
The farms may also be built in or near the ocean.

Wind Energy

Wind energy is another kind of renewable energy. People have used wind energy for thousands of years. Early **explorers** caught wind in their ships' sails to travel across the seas. Scientists today have learned how to use wind energy to meet our growing needs.

Wind **turbines** are used to catch the wind's energy. First, wind turns the large blades on top of a turbine. The moving blades spin a small rod inside the long pole that holds the turbine. This turning rod joins to a machine called a **generator**, which makes electricity. Wind farms have many tall turbines. Together, they create lots of electricity.

Water Power

Water can make a form of renewable energy called hydroelectric power. Most hydroelectric power is produced when moving water turns a large turbine with bucketlike blades. The turning turbine is joined to a generator, which creates electricity.

Hydroelectric plants use dams, or large walls that hold water back. Dams are generally built in rivers. A dam can control the flow of water, so hydroelectric power can be made as needed. The Hoover Dam, on the Colorado River, supplies electricity to Nevada, Arizona, and California.

DID YOU KNOW?

Geothermal energy is another form of renewable energy. Geothermal energy uses heat from the center of Earth to make electricity. There are more than 200 geothermal energy plants in the world.

Breaking Atoms

Everything in our world is made of tiny parts called **atoms**. Large amounts of energy are stored inside atoms. When an atom is broken apart, the energy inside comes out as heat. The energy made by breaking up atoms is called nuclear energy.

In nuclear power plants, people use the heat that is created when atoms are broken apart to make electricity. About one-fifth of the electricity used in the United States comes from nuclear energy. Atoms of a metal called uranium are used to make nuclear energy. This is because uranium atoms come apart more easily than other atoms do.

DID YOU KNOW?

Nuclear energy plants make lots of electricity, but they also produce waste that can hurt people. This waste is stored carefully so it will not leak out near people.

Energy for the Years Ahead

We must continue to conserve energy and to search for energy to power our world in new places. Lately, scientists found a great energy supply by learning how to make new **biofuels** from plants. Today, cars and trucks often burn biofuels mixed with gasoline. The most common biofuel, called ethanol, is made from corn.

Surprisingly, scientists have also found energy in waves. A wave power plant off Portugal's coast takes energy from waves and turns it into electricity. Maybe you will find a new energy supply when you grow up. Who knows, we might even make all of our energy from trash someday!

GLOSSARY

atoms (A-temz) The smallest parts of any element. Elements are the most basic kind of matter.

biofuels (by-oh-FYOO-elz) Kinds of energy made from once-living things that died in the recent past.

conserve (kun-SERV) To keep something from being wasted or used up.

electricity (ih-lek-TRIH-suh-tee) Power that produces light, heat, or movement.

explorers (ek-SPLOR-erz) People who travel and look for new land.

generator (JEH-neh-ray-tur) A machine that makes electricity.

millions (MIL-yunz) Thousands of thousands.

pollute (puh-LOOT) To hurt with certain kinds of bad matter.

scientists (SY-un-tists) People who study the world.

sources (SORS-ez) The places from which things start.

temperature (TEM-pur-chur) How hot or cold something is.

turbines (TER-bynz) Motors that turn by a flow of water or wind.

INDEX

A
asthma, 11
atom(s), 21

B
bike, 13
biofuels, 22

C
coal, 7, 9
computers, 5
corn, 22

D
dam(s), 19
deserts, 11

H
Hoover Dam, 19

N
natural gas, 7
nuclear energy, 21

P
polar bears, 11

S
solar panels, 15
spaceships, 15
Sun, 9, 15

U
United States, 5, 7
uranium, 21

W
wave(s), 22
wind farms, 17
wind turbines, 17

WEB SITES

Due to the changing nature of Internet links, PowerKids Press has developed an online list of Web sites related to the subject of this book. This site is updated regularly. Please use this link to access the list:
www.powerkidslinks.com/ourpl/energy/